WRITER
MARK GRUENWALD

PENCILS AND CO-PLOTTER
KIERON DWYER

INKER
DANNY BULANADI

COLORS
BOB SHAREN
GREG WRIGHT
MARC SIRY

LETTERS
JACK MORELLI

EDITOR
RALPH MACCHIO

BOOK DESIGN
JOE KAUFMAN

REPRINT EDITOR
MIKE ROCKWITZ

EDITOR IN CHIEF
TOM DEFALCO

CAPTAIN AMERICA®**: THE BLOODSTONE HUNT.** Originally published in magazine form as Captain America #'s 357-364. Published by MARVEL COMICS, 387 PARK AVENUE SOUTH, NEW YORK, NY 10016. Copyright © 1989, 1993 Marvel Entertainment Group, Inc. All rights reserved. CAPTAIN AMERICA and all prominent characters appearing herein and the distinctive names and likenesses thereof are trademarks of MARVEL ENTERTAINMENT GROUP, INC. No part of this book may be printed or reproduced in any manner without the written permission of the publisher. Printed in the U.S.A. ISBN #0-87135-972-3. First Printing June, 1993. GST #R127032852

10 9 8 7 6 5 4 3 2 1

THE AMERICAN MUSEUM OF NATURAL HISTORY IN NEW YORK CITY...

TRUTH

KNOWLEDGE

COME. ZIS WAY!

WHOOO

VOILA! ZEES IS IT!

KAFF! KAFF!

IT *IS*, MR. ZARAN. UNBELIEVABLY VALUABLE.

QUE?

HERR *BATROC*...ZARAN... *MACHETE*... THIS IS MY ASSOCIATE, *TRISTRAM MICAWBER.* HE IS A PSYCHIC DETECTIVE.

↑ THIS END U

FRAGILE

THE SKELETON, AS THE BARON TOLD YOU, BE-LONGED TO A MAN NAMED *ULYSSES BLOOD-STONE.* HE HAD SOME RENOWN AS A HUNTER OF... *MONSTERS.*

LITTLE ELSE IS KNOWN ABOUT HIM... TILL *NOW.*

"I SEE... THE DAWN OF THE *HUMAN SPECIES*...

"I SEE...HIM DRESSED IN ANIMAL SKINS, HUNTING A *WOOLY MAMMOTH.* EVEN 20,000 YEARS AGO BLOODSTONE DISPLAYED A PROCLIVITY FOR SLAYING *BEHEMOTHS!*

"*NOW* I SEE... A *METEORITE* FALLING FROM THE SKY.

"*THE* FEARLESS HUNTER LEAVES THE SAFETY OF HIS TRIBE'S CAMPFIRE TO *INVESTIGATE*...

"I SEE... A TENTACLE-FACED *EXTRATERRES-TRIAL* --

"-- AND THE STAR-BORN *GEMSTONE* THAT WOULD BECOME THE HUNTER'S NAMESAKE!

"I SEE... BLOODSTONE *SHATTERING* THE JEWEL WITH HIS FLINT *SPEAR-TIP*...

"... SOMEHOW SENSING THE *EVIL* INHERENT IN THE STONE!"

"I SEE... ONE OF THE EXPLODING FRAGMENTS OF THE BLOODSTONE EMBEDDING ITSELF INTO THE HUNTER'S *STERNUM*...

"THE BLOODSTONE HAD MADE ULYSSES *IMMORTAL*.

"DOWN THROUGH THE *CENTURIES*, HE STALKED AND SLAYED *MONSTERS*.

"I SEE HIM NOW... JUST A *FEW YEARS* BACK...

"...HUNTING BEHEMOTHS AS HE HAS EVER...

"BUT THEN... HE WAS TAKEN CAPTIVE BY A GROUP CALLING ITSELF THE *CONSPIRACY*. A DEMENTED SURGEON REMOVED THE BLOODSTONE FROM HIS CHEST--

"...AND USED IT TO CREATE A *CRYSTALLINE MONSTER!* ON THE VERGE OF DYING, BLOOD-STONE CONFRONTED THE CREATURE...

"--AND *SHATTERED* IT! ULYSSES BLOODSTONE THEN *COLLAPSED!*

"THE *MILLENNIA* HE CHEATED DEATH FINALLY TAKING THEIR *TOLL* ON HIM!"

THE POLICE TOOK HIS *REMAINS* INTO CUSTODY AND EVENTUALLY TURNED THEM OVER TO THE *MUSEUM*...

AND THE *GEMS*-- WHAT OF *THEM*?!?

THEY *VANISHED!*

BUT YOU CAN HELP ME *FIND* THEM-- CAN'T YOU, HERR MICAWBER?

I BELIEVE SO!

A CHOICE, MEIN HERREN! EITHER I PAY YOU EACH *TEN* THOUSAND FOR THE *SKELETON* OR A *HUNDRED* THOUSAND EACH FOR EVERY *BLOOD-STONE* YOU HELP ME RECOVER!

TELL ME MORE, MON AMI!!

WHAT?

Shhh!

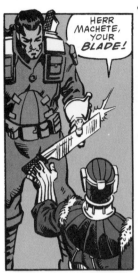

HERR MACHETE, YOUR *BLADE!*

HACK

▲ THIS

THERE! THE SECTION OF THE *RIBCAGE* IN WHICH THE *BLOOD-STONE* WAS ONCE IMBEDDED. THIS IS ALL WE WILL *NEED!*

HERR MICAWBER?

YES... YES... I CAN FEEL THE *VIBRATIONS* OF THE BLOOD-STONE FRAGMENTS. THERE ARE *FIVE* OF THEM... OUR *DIVINING ROD* WILL LEAD US STRAIGHT TO THEM!

WUNDERBAR!

THE SKELETON IS OF NO FURTHER *USE* TO US. DUMP THE WOMAN'S *BODY* ON TOP OF IT, THEN NAIL IT *SHUT!*

SUCH A WASTE!

FRAGILE

WE WILL *DISPOSE* OF THE BODIES WHERE NO ONE SHALL EVER *FIND* THEM AGAIN!

LET US BE *OFF!*

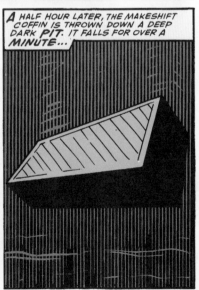

A HALF HOUR LATER, THE MAKESHIFT COFFIN IS THROWN DOWN A DEEP DARK *PIT.* IT FALLS FOR OVER A MINUTE...

SIGNAL'S GETTING STRONGER THAN *EVER!*

I CAN'T IMAGINE HOW SHE EVER GOT HERSELF IN TROUBLE THIS *DEEP.*

BiP BiP BiP

WHAT'S ALL THAT *NOISE?*

WHOO

AN *UP-DRAFT*-- FROM THIS *PIT!*

ODD. A HOLE IN THE *CEILING* OF THE CAVE DIRECTLY OVER THE HOLE IN THIS *FLOOR.*

WELL I'LL BE--! I SEE A PINPRICK OF *LIGHT* UP THERE!

IT COULDN'T LEAD STRAIGHT TO THE *SURFACE* COULD IT?

AND WHAT'S *DOWN* THERE?

COULDN'T TELL IF I HEARD THAT STONE HIT *BOTTOM.* MAYBE IT JUST GOT LOST IN THE HOWL OF THE *WIND.*

I'D HATE TO THINK I'D DISCOVERED THE PROVER-BIAL *BOTTOM-LESS PIT!*

SIGNAL SEEMS TO BE COMING FROM *BELOW.*

SEE HOW FAR DOWN MY *ROPE* WILL LET ME GO!

Whew. WHAT AN *INCREDIBLE WIND!*

I FEEL ALMOST *WEIGHTLESS* HAVE TO GET A *TOEHOLD* TO KEEP FROM BEING BLOWN BACK UP THE SHAFT!

WHOOOO

MY FOOT *HIT* SOMETHING!

LATER... BLOODSTONE, ULYSSES... NOT MUCH ON HIM. HE WAS AN ADVENTURER WHO BILLED HIMSELF AS A "MONSTER-HUNTER".

THE GEM HE WORE ON HIS CHEST... APPARENTLY WAS A MYSTICAL POWER-STONE... NO MENTION OF WHERE THOSE DEAD PEOPLE IN THE CHAMBER FIT IN.

THIS IS FABULOUS, SITTING HERE IN CAP'S PRIVATE OFFICE HELPING HIM WORK--!

HEY, CAPARINO CHECK THIS OUT!

WHAT IS IT, FABIAN?

I ANALYZED THIS SKULL LIKE YOU ASKED ME--

--AND SURE ENOUGH, THIS THING IS GIVING OFF SOME WEIRD ENERGY.. THE COMPUTERS ARE STILL TRYING TO IDENTIFY IT!

ANYWAY, I HOOKED UP A RADIOMETER TO IT, AND BOY HOWDY, LOOK! THIS BONE-DOME HAS A REAL STRONG ATTRACTION TO SOMETHING SOUTH-SOUTHEAST OF HERE!

THE BLOOD STONE..?

FABIAN, I KNEW THERE WAS A REASON I HIRED YOU!

HEY, WHERE'RE YOU--?

I WANT TO CHECK OUT THE SOURCE OF THIS RADIATION. IF BATROC IS BEING PAID BIG MONEY TO FIND THE STONE. I WANT TO KEEP IT FROM HIM!

BACK ON THE AIRSTRIP...

AH, HE'S BACK.

COME TO SEE THE SHIP, CAPTAIN?

NO, MICHAEL, I'VE COME TO FLY HER. SHE FLIGHTWORTHY?

MMM-MMH! LOOK AT THAT TUSHIE MOVE!

DIAMONDBACK, BEFORE I LET YOU TAG ALONG, I WANT YOU TO PROMISE THERE WON'T BE ANY FUNNY BUSINESS LIKE LAST TIME WE WORKED TOGETHER! *

SCOUT'S HONOR!

WHY, YES. THE COLONEL HERE'S SPENT ALL AFTERNOON--

*DAILY BUGLE PUBLISHER J. JONAH JAMESON. --REPORTER RALF

ROGER, CAPTAIN.

NO, NOTHING MORE *DEFINITE*. BUT I'LL LET YOU KNOW IF WE *OVERSHOOT*, OKAY?

TWO HOURS LATER...

WE'RE ABOUT TWENTY MILES SOUTH OF THE *EQUATOR*... THAT'S THE *AMAZON RIVER* DOWN THERE...

THE COMPASS NEEDLE ON THIS MAKESHIFT *BLOODSTONE-DETECTOR* JUST DID A *360*. WE JUST OVERSHOT, COLONEL.

I'LL TURN THIS BABY *AROUND*. DON'T SEE A CLEARING IN THE *RAINFOREST* BIG ENOUGH TO *LAND*, EVEN WITH *VTOL*.

LOOKS LIKE WE'LL HAVE TO *JUMP*.

YOU EVER USE A *PARACHUTE* BEFORE, DIAMOND?

OH, SURE-- *LOTS* OF TIMES...

OH, NO--!

I... HATE... THIS!!

KSSHH

EASY NOW!

WRASHH

DIAMONDBACK!

DON'T SEE ANY CORDS OR VINES AROUND HER NECK--!

DIAMOND--?

NNhhh...

OOOEEE!

OOAAHH!

YOU'LL BE OKAY, DIAMOND. WE'RE ALMOST DOWN!

S-SORRY, CAP... I HIT A BRANCH AND--AND--

IT'S TOO LATE FOR ME TO LEAVE YOU BEHIND. I'LL NEVER FIND YOU IN ALL THIS HEAVY GROWTH.

I'LL BE OKAY, CAP-- REALLY!

Sheeze! I WAS HOPING TO SHOW HIM WHAT A GREAT TEAM WE MAKE... BUT I SURE AM OFF TO A LOUSY START!

HOW AM I SUPPOSED TO KEEP UP WITH A GUY THIS GUNG-HO?

I SHOULD'VE STAYED IN AUSTRALIA WITH THE X-MEN!*

SKRASH

FIFTEEN MINUTES LATER...

WHOAAA!!

DIAMOND??

OH, CAP, I'M *SORRY!* MY HEEL MUST'VE GOTTEN *STUCK*... I FEEL SO...

IT'S OKAY.

LOOK WHAT YOU TRIPPED ON -- AN *INCA IDOL!*

OH-- *HA!* ACTUALLY I DID THAT ON PUR--

Shhh... I HEAR SOME-THING--!

CAP--??

THESE MEN ARE DRESSED LIKE *INCAS!* BUT THE LAST OF THE INCAS WERE SUPPOSED TO HAVE DIED OUT OVER A HUNDRED YEARS AGO!

WE COME IN PEACE.

NO ANSWER, WISH I KNEW PORTUGESE, BRAZIL'S NATIONAL LANGUAGE.

I COULD *FIGHT* MY WAY OUT... BUT NOT WITHOUT PUTTING DIAMONDBACK IN *JEOPARDY!*

NO TELLING *HOW* MANY MORE OF THEM COULD BE HIDING IN THE *TREES.*

CAP, WHAT SHOULD WE *DO?*

PLAY ALONG. THEY MAY PROVE HELPFUL IN OUR SEARCH.

SOON...

A PYRAMID. APPARENTLY OUR *DESTINATION!*

HOPE THEIR *CHIEFTAIN* SPEAKS SOMETHING OTHER THAN INCAN.

AND EQUALLY IMPORTANT, I HOPE HE KNOWS SOMETHING ABOUT A CERTAIN *SCARLET GEM!*

I JUST *THOUGHT* OF SOMETHING. WHAT IF BATROC AND CREW HAVE *BEATEN* US HERE, AND HAVE FORCED THIS ANCIENT TRIBE TO DO THEIR *BIDDING?*

COULD THEY HAVE LEARNED WE'RE COMING-- OR DO THESE MEN TAKE *ALL* STRANGERS PRISONER?

SHOULD FIND OUT SOON ENOUGH!

NO SIGN OF *BATROC.* THAT'S A RELIEF, I SUPPOSE!

I WISH I KNEW WHAT THESE PEOPLE WERE *SAYING.*

⟨O LEADER! MORE STRANGERS!⟩

⟨BRING THEM FORTH!⟩

TRANSLATED FROM THE INCAN. --MR. FLUENCY

AREN'T INCAS INTO *HUMAN* SACRIFICES?

SHOULDN'T WE--?

THE OPPORTUNITY HASN'T COME UP YET, DIAMOND. STAY *COOL.*

< RAISE THE *WHEEL OF DEATH!* >

DIAMOND, THAT *JEWEL* GLITTERING ON THE CHIEF'S HEADDRESS-- WHAT'S IT LOOK LIKE?

OH, WOW-- I'LL BET IT'S THE *BLOOD-STONE!*

RRRRRR

CAP! *LOOK!*

BATROC, ZEMO, MACHETE, AND ZARAN-- *PRISONERS!!*

FOR A MOMENT I THOUGHT THEY WERE *DEAD!* TIME TO *MOVE*--!

ZAIR, BARON-- OUR *RESCUERS!*

LET US HOPE SO, *AMIGO!*

FFFT

DIAMOND-- A!!EGK!

FFFT

BLOWDART... IN THE BACK OF THE *NECK* ...

IT'S *CURARE,* CAPTAIN, YOU'LL BE *PARALYZED* IN *SECONDS!*

‹ PLACE THEM UPON THE *WHEEL OF DEATH!* ›*

*TRANSLATED FROM THE INCAN.

C-CAP-- I CAN'T EVEN--

WELL, BARON, IF ZEY MEAN TO *SACRIFICE* US, AT LEAST OUR *GREATEST ENEMY* WEEL *DIE WEETH US!*

Oh, SHUT UP, BATROC!

CONCENTRATE ON *ESCAPE!*

I'M STARTING TO FEEL THE *CURARE* WEARING OFF! IF THESE *RED-SKINS* WILL ONLY GIVE US A FEW MINUTES *MORE!*

BARON, YOUR *BAJO,* FRIEND, *MICAWBER,* IS STILL AT THE *SHIP.* WHEN WILL HE COME *LOOKING* FOR US?

I DO NOT *KNOW.*

CONCENTRATE--! GET THAT *HEART* BEATING *FASTER,* PUMPING *HARDER,* YOU GOOD-FOR-NOTHING *WARHORSE!*

THAT'S ALL OF THEM IN THE *IMMEDIATE VICINITY!* BUT AT LEAST HALF OF THEM *FLED!*

AND *ONE* OF THEM HAS MY *SHIELD!*

THERE!

HAVE TO MAKE THIS SPIN *JUST RIGHT!*

THEN MAKE *TRACKS,* MAN!

WHOULP!!

Whew! THAT WAS CLOSE! IF THIS *SKULL-GIZMO* SHATTERED, WE'D NEVER BE ABLE TO TRACK DOWN THE *OTHER FOUR* BLOODSTONE FRAGMENTS!

NOW TO SEE TO *DIA-MOND!*

WHAT IN--? BARON ZEMO AND BATROC'S BRIGADE-- *GONE--!!*

DIAMONDBACK--

--WHAT *HAPPENED?* WHERE'D THEY *GO?*

CAAAAP... YOU CAME *BACK...*

WHAT HAPPENED TO ZEMO AND HIS CREW..?

ZARAN... SPEAR...

ZARAN MUST'VE GOTTEN HIS HANDS ON A SPEAR AND PRIED OPEN HIS SHACKLES. GREAT. THEY'RE GONE, AND THEY TOOK THE HELMET WITH THE BLOODSTONE!

HOW'D THEY GET PAST ME WITHOUT-- HMM?

I SEE SOMETHING!

Wheeee!

A HIDDEN EXIT... JUST MY LUCK.

KRMM

DON'T HEAR ANY FOOTSTEPS OR BREATHING. THEY MUST BE LONG GONE!

THE PROVERBIAL LIGHT AT THE END OF THE TUNNEL.

WHAT'S THAT FAINT WHINE?

ZEMO HAD AN AIRCRAFT WAITING!

BLAST IT ALL!

I'LL SIGNAL MY PILOT. THERE'S STILL A CHANCE WE CAN OVERTAKE THE ZEMO SHIP!

WHT

SEVERAL HUNDRED METERS BELOW...

WHAT'S THAT HUGE *LIGHT SHAPE* DOWN THERE?

IS IT POSSIBLE WE *BEAT* ZEMO HERE? *NOT LIKELY* GIVEN HIS HEAD START...

AN *AIRLINER!* HMM, I REMEMBER SOMETHING ABOUT A *PASSENGER JET* BEING LOST IN THE BERMUDA TRIANGLE A FEW YEARS AGO!

ACCORDING TO THE "SKULLOMETER", THE BLOODSTONE'S *INSIDE!* I WONDER IF IT HAD ANYTHING TO DO WITH THE *CRASH* OR IT WAS MERELY A *COINCIDENCE?*

NO SIGN OF *ZEMO'S CREW* AS OF YET--

WHOOPS! SPOKE TOO SOON! *BATROC, MACHETE,* AND *ZARAN!*

CAPTAIN AMERICA! HA-HA!

SPOOANG

HARPOON-GUN! SINGLE BOLT LOADING. CAN'T SEE HOW MANY *SPARES* HE'S GOT--

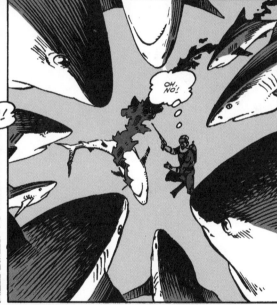

THE SHARK'S BLOOD IS GETTING HIS BROTHERS OFF MY CASE--

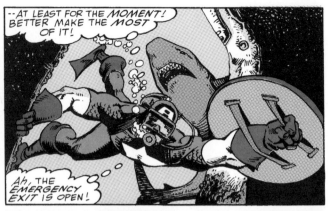

--AT LEAST FOR THE *MOMENT!* BETTER MAKE THE *MOST* OF IT!

Ah, THE *EMERGENCY EXIT* IS OPEN!

TOO OPEN, UN-FORTUNATELY!

GOT TO MAKE IT UP TO THE *COCKPIT* WHERE BATROC AND CROWD ARE LOCKED AWAY BEFORE--

--BEFORE *THIS* HAPPENS!

EASY NOW, SHARKY--

--NO *JOSTLING!* PLENTY OF ROOM IN HERE FOR US BOTH!

MEANWHILE, SEVERAL HUNDRED FEET ABOVE...

SPOT YOUR FRIEND'S BOAT YET, MS. LEIGHTON?

NO.... NOT YET.

WHAT A MAROON! BUYING MY STORY THAT I LOST TRACK OF THE YACHT I SCUBA-DOVE FROM!

NO, HONEY-- IT'S BARON ZEMO'S BOAT CAP TOLD ME TO SCOUT AROUND FOR...

... AND CONSIDERING HOW LITTLE USE TO CAP I'VE BEEN SO FAR, HERE'S WHERE THIS LITTLE OL' DIAMOND-BACK STARTS EARNING HER KEEP!

AWWRIGHT!!! THE REFLECTION IN THAT WINDOW-- IT LOOKS LIKE ZEMO'S FUNKY HEADGEAR!

I THINK I'VE FOUND HIM-- UH, THEM, MR. DURER!

WOULD YOU LIKE ME TO--

YOU'VE DONE PLENTY!

THANKS!

BYE!

SPLOOSH!

BELOW...

BATROC'S GASH DID IT-- THE SHARKS ARE HAVING A *FEEDING FRENZY!*

STILL CAN'T YANK MY *SHIELD* LOOSE, THOUGH!

I CAN DO *NO MORE* FOR ZEE CAPITAN WITHOUT JEOPARDIZING MY *OWN* WORTHLESS HIDE!

I HOPE EET WAS *ENOUGH!*

ONE *SIDE,* BATROC!

LET ME GO UP FIRST!

BARONN! WE'RE BACK! AND WE HAVE ZEE *BLOOD-STONE!*

SHUT *UP,* BAT! SOMETHING'S HAPPENED *HERE!*

I HAPPENED HERE, BOYS! REMEMBER *ME?* ZEMO AND THE *DWARF* DO!

NOW I WANT YOU TO ALL PUT YOUR *HANDS* UP HIGH WHERE I CAN SEE THEM, *CAPEESH!?*

NOW, WHO HAS THE BLOOD-STONE FRAGMENT?

TELL ME OR THE BARON HERE GETS A COUPLE DOZEN NEW *EYEHOLES* IN THIS FUNKY MASK OF HIS!

I DO, MADAM-OISELLE, IN MY BELT.

GOOD! TAKE IT *OUT-- VERY SLOWLY!*

DON'T *DO* IT! SHE HAS *ALREADY* TAKEN MY *OTHER* TWO FRAG-MENTS!

MACHETE -- SEE TO M'SIEU MICAWBER! ZARAN -- HELP ZEE BARONN FIND ZEE *FRAGMENT* I THREW!

WHOAAAAH! BATROC -- YOU ARE THE *WORST* --

VROOM

NEVER MIND -- I'VE *FOUND* IT! THE PIECE THAT SHE-DOG *DROPPED!*

THAT MAKES *THREE!*

VAS IS DAS?!

SHE *STOLE* THE TWO FRAGMENTS IN THE CASE WHILE MY BACK WAS TURNED! THAT -- THAT --

EASY, BARON. WHAT DO YOU WANT US TO DO? TURN BACK AND DREDGE FOR HER *BODY?*

A NAUTICAL MILE BACK...

I THINK I'VE MANAGED TO SHAKE THOSE -- MY GOD -- *DIAMONDBACK?!*

SHE'S *UNCONSCIOUS* -- *BLEEDING* FROM HER SHOULDER! HOW LONG HAS SHE BEEN *DOWN* HERE?

STEADY NOW, GIRL, BREATHE THROUGH MY *AIRHOSE!*

WE MADE IT!

AND THERE'S MY FLAGSHIP-- RESPONDING TO MY BELT- TRANSMITTER!

HOLD ON, DIA- MOND! I PROMISE I'LL DO A MORE THOROUGH JOB OF GETTING ALL THE WATER OUT OF YOUR LUNGS AS SOON AS WE'RE ON A FIRM SURFACE!

And...

CAPTAIN -- IS SHE?

DON'T KNOW YET, COLONEL!

PFAUUGH!

DIAMOND--??

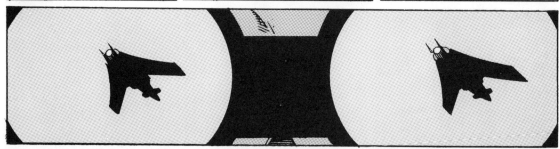

INSIDE THE FLAGSHIP SOME TIME LATER.

NNNHHH... C--CAP--??

EASY, DIAMOND... EVERYTHING'S OKAY, THOUGH YOU HAD ME WORRIED FOR A MOMENT THERE!

I DID? YOU WERE WORRIED ABOUT... ME?

SURE. SO WHAT HAPPENED? HOW'D YOU WIND UP FLOATING IN THE DRINK?

WELL, I LOCATED ZEMO'S BOAT LIKE YOU WANTED ME TO... GOT THE DROP ON ZEMO...

...AND GRABBED THE BRIEFCASE WHERE HE WAS STORING HIS BLOOD-STONE FRAGMENTS.

UNFORTUNATELY, WHEN HIS HIRELINGS RETURNED, THEY GOT THE DROP ON ME!

WASN'T A TOTAL LOSS, THOUGH!

LOOK!

I SWIPED THE TWO STONES OUT OF HIS CASE!

SURELY I DESERVE A KISS FOR THAT!

DIAMOND--!

I WAS JUST KIDDING... SHEESH, CAN'T A GIRL MAKE A JOKE AROUND YOU?

I DO APPRECIATE WHAT YOU'VE ACCOMPLISHED, DIAMOND,

BUT SINCE YOU'VE BEEN INJURED, I WANT YOU TO SIT OUT THE REST OF THE MISSION!

NO WAY, CAP! THIS IS ONLY A FLESH WOUND! I'VE HAD FAR WORSE! I'M IN WITH YOU TO THE BITTER END!

WHAT IS OUR NEXT STOP ANYWAY?

"ACCORDING TO OUR BLOODSTONE-DETECTOR... EGYPT!"

AND SOON...

OKAY, COLONEL, TAKE 'ER BACK *UP* AND KEEP AN EYE OUT FOR ZEMO'S SHIP!

WITH ANY *LUCK*, WE *BEAT* HIM HERE THIS TIME!

LOOK-- A *STAIRWAY* LEADING BENEATH THE SAND. THE SIGNAL SEEMS TO BE COMING FROM *THERE!*

WOW! FROM UNDER THE *SEA* TO UNDER THE *SAND* IN A MATTER OF *HOURS!*

A GIRL SURE GETS TO SEE THE *WORLD* HANGING AROUND YOU, CAP!

I'M *SERIOUS*, DIAMOND. PROMISE ME, IF YOUR INJURY STARTS TO BOTHER YOU, YOU'LL *TELL* ME SO I CAN SEND YOU BACK TO THE SHIP!

SURE, CAP...

AND LET YOU THINK I'M A *WIMP*? *NEVER!*

WOW! *LOOK* AT THIS STUFF! THESE BLOODSTONES SURE MANAGED GET THEMSELVES INTO SOME PRETTY WILD, OUT-OF-THE WAY PLACES!

YES... *THAT*, AND WHAT ZEMO INTENDS TO *DO* WITH THE BLOODSTONE FRAGMENTS ONCE HE GETS HOLD OF THEM, ARE THE TWO *BIG* MYSTERIES OF THIS WHOLE SHEBANG!

HOW'S THE *SHOULDER* DOING?

GREAT!

KLMPP

SSSSS

EEOOWW!

I DON'T *KNOW* ABOUT THIS. I THINK I CAN MAKE THE *15-FOOT* STANDING HIGH JUMP--

--BUT CAN *DIAMOND'S ARM* TAKE MY *240 POUNDS* !?

IT'S MY *BEST OPTION* AT THIS POINT!

SSS

SSS

THE *TRAPDOOR* IS BEGINNING TO *CLOSE!*

AM I--??

UHAAAGGHH!!

KRIK

MMF! MMF! MMF!

I'M UP--

Oh Oh Oh Oh!

KRNCH

--EXCEPT FOR MY *SHIELD!*

AT THAT MOMENT, OUTSIDE...

HOLD IT, ZEMO! THE DIVING ROD IS GOING LOCO! THAT PYRAMID BELOW MUST HOUSE THE NEXT BLOODSTONE FRAGMENT!

THE HATED CAPTAIN AMERICA UNDOUBTEDLY BEAT US HERE. WE WILL LET HIM DO THE DIRTY WORK FOR US THIS TIME--

--WHEN HE COMES OUT OF THE TOMB YOU WILL AMBUSH HIM! VERSTEHEN SIE DAS?

PARDON, BARONN, BUT WHY SHOULD WE TAKE ZEE THREE FRAGMENTS HE HAS FROM HIM HERE? WOULD IT NOT BE BETTER TO WAIT UNTIL HE HAS ZEE FIFTH AND FINAL PIECE?

ZEN HE COULD DO ALL ZEE DIRTY WORK--

NO, BATROC, IT IS TOO RISKY TO LET HIM HAVE FOUR FRAGMENTS WHILE I HAVE BUT ONE!

AND IF YOU THREE FAIL ME, YOU WILL STILL HAVE ONE MORE CHANCE!

NOW GO! AND DON'T LET THE WOMAN GET AWAY THIS TIME!

ZEE BARONN TREATS US LIKE INCOMPETENTS, EH, MACHETE?

HE CAN TREAT US ANY WAY HE WANTS AS LONG AS HE COMES THROUGH WITH THE DINERO FOR THE FIVE GEM-PIECES WE'RE DELIVERING!

THAT WOULD APPEAR TO BE ZEE ENTRANCE, NON?

I WONDAIR IF ZEE CAPITAN IS INDEED *WITHIN ZESE*--

HOLD IT RIGHT *THERE*, BAT. YOU HEARD ZEMO--NO *HELPING* EL CAPITAN THIS TIME!

I *TOLD* YOU, I ONLY AIDED HIM *LAST* TIME IN ORDER TO CLEAR *US* A WAY PAST THE *SHARKS!*

SURE YOU DID, BATSY. I THINK YOU'RE GOING *SWEET* ON THE AMERICAN AFTER ALL THESE YEARS!

YOU--!

HEY-- WHAT--??

FWUMP

M'SIEU ZARAN-- NEVAIR CALL BATROC *ANYZING* BUT A LADIES'MAN--

--IF YOU *WEESH* TO KEEP A *FULL* SET OF *TEETH* COMPRENDS?

CRAZY JUMPING BEAN--!

INSIDE THE TOMB...

THERE'S NO WAY DIAMOND COULD'VE GOTTEN UP AND WALKED *PAST* ME--

--NOR DO I SEE ANY *PASSAGEWAY* BEYOND THIS CHAMBER!

THERE MUST BE A HIDDEN *DOOR* SOMEWHERE.

THIS PLACE IS PRETTY *AIRTIGHT.* IF THERE WERE ONLY MORE *DUST* I MIGHT...

--WHAT'S *THIS?*

A SHRED OF OLD *CLOTH...* LIKE A *MUMMY WRAPPING!*

DIAMOND'S GROAN WAS JUST THE *DISTRACTION* I NEEDED!

WHTHUDD

JABBING HIS WIND-PIPE WASN'T ENOUGH-- MAYBE *SMASHING* IT--??

HUUP! GUESS ONE GOOD *SORE THROAT*-- HUUP! --DESERVES *ANOTHER.* HMH?

GURK.

DIAMOND ??

YOU ALL RIGHT ?

I FEEL *GREAT,* CAP!

NO PAIN IN YOUR *WOUNDED SHOULDER*?

NONE!

HMMM.

YOU WERE TRYING TO *HELP* HER, EH?

WHY?

YIKES! A--A *MUMMY!*

Uhrrr... <WOMAN'S BODY... FEELS GEM ...NEED...>

UH-UH, CAP. I HEARD A FEW WORDS OF MODERN EGYPTIAN--

SO YOU CAN DO BETTER THAN GROAN.

STILL CAN'T TELL WHAT YOU'RE TRYING TO SAY, THOUGH. MUST BE SPEAKING SOME ANCIENT EGYPTIAN DIALECT.

--A LANGUAGE I HAPPEN TO BE ACQUAINTED WITH THANKS TO MY SERPENT SOCIETY TEAMMATE, THE ASP!

SAYS HIS NAME'S N'KANTU... HE'S SAYING SOMETHING ABOUT THE RED GEM... HE HAS ONE, I THINK... SOMEHOW SENSED I HAD TOUCHED OTHERS LIKE IT...

WHAT'S HE WANT THEM FOR?

UH, I THINK HE THINKS THEY'LL RE-STORE HIM--DEMUMMIFY HIM, I GUESS.

TELL HIM THAT THERE ARE EVIL MEN COMING WHO WILL STOP AT NOTHING TO STEAL HIS GEM. HE CAN TAKE HIS CHANCES WITH THEM OR GIVE IT TO US.

IF HE DOES, TELL HIM I PROMISE TO RETURN ALL FIVE FRAGMENTS TO HIM--

--PROVIDED THEY TRULY TURN OUT TO HAVE RESTORATIVE POWERS.

AND, AFTER A PAINSTAKING TRANSLATION...

HE JUST SAID THAT IF YOU'RE LYING TO HIM, HE WILL SPEND THE REST OF HIS IMMORTAL LIFE HUNTING YOU DOWN!

TELL HIM I NEVER LIE.

THANK YOU. NOW IF YOU HAPPEN TO KNOW ANY BACK WAY OUT OF HERE?

ABOVE...

WHAT IS TAKING THEM SO LONG?

INCOMPETENTS!

IF MY BROKEN NECK WERE ONLY HEALED, I'D -- VAS??

HERR MICAWBER-- YOU'VE AWAKENED. LET ME GIVE YOU SOMETHING TO DRINK!

WH-WHAT... HAP... HAPPENED?

THAT SHE-DOG DIAMONDBACK STRUCK YOU IN THE FOREHEAD WITH A PROJECTILE, MY PSYCHIC FRIEND... YOU'VE SUFFERED A BAD CON-CUSSION... THIS IS THE FIRST YOU'VE STIRRED IN--

ZEEMOHH...

H-HAD VISION, ZEMO-- SOMEONE... SOMEONE ELSE WANTS THE B-BLOODSTONES... TWO OTHERS...

WHO?

WHO??

Uhhhh!...

ACH--! THAT TOLD ME NOTHING!

SOMEONE ELSE WANTS THE BLOOD-STONES -- BAH! LET THEM!

NOTHING--NO ONE-- WILL STAND IN MY WAY! BY THE BLESSED BONES OF MY FATHER, THE BLOODSTONES SHALL BE MINE! AND WITH THEM, I SHALL ATTAIN MY HEART'S FONDEST DESIRES!

EVEN HIGHER ABOVE...

THE WAY HE'S CIRCLING THE *PYRAMID*--

THIS FLAGSHIP'S *STEALTH SCREENS* MUST BE PRETTY DARN GOOD THAT HE CAN'T *SEE* ME HOVERING A COUPLE OF HUNDRED FEET ABOVE HIM!

BE FUN TO EN-GAGE THE *RED BARON* IN A LITTLE *DOG-FIGHT!*

BUT CAP'S ORDERS ARE SIMPLY TO KEEP ZEMO UNDER *SURVEILLANCE* AND AWAIT HIS *PICKUP* CALL!

--BARON *ZEMO* MUST BE GETTING MIGHTY *IMPATIENT!*

WONDER HOW OUR *TWO BLOODSTONES* ARE DOING?

SOMETHING ABOUT THEM *FASCINATES* ME!

AS IF I CAN'T GUESS *WHAT*--

REMINDS ME OF THE *MOON-STONE* I ONCE WORE...

--THAT ONCE WORE *ME*...

"...WHEN *COLONEL JOHN JAMESON*, USAF, BECAME THE SAVAGE MAN-BEAST THE WORLD CAME TO KNOW AS THE *MAN-WOLF!*

GOT TO... PUT THESE... *AWAY*... STOP PLAY-ING WITH THEM--

THE MOONSTONE IS *GONE*. THAT PART OF MY LIFE...

...IS ALL *BEHIND* ME!

HEH HEH!

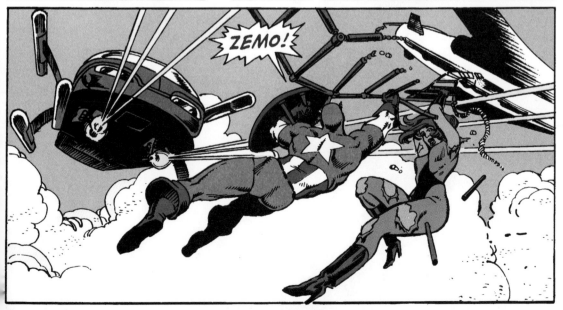

A SHORT TIME LATER, BELOW...

HURRY, MES AMI, I CANNOT WAIT TO SEE ZEE BARON'S FACE WHEN WE SHOW HIM OUR PRIZE!

I THINK YOU'VE BEEN OUT IN THE SUN TOO LONG, BATROC! HOW CAN YOU TELL ZEMO'S EXPRESSION THROUGH THAT HOOD OF HIS?

BARONN-- VOILA! WE HAVE IT-- ZEE THIRD GEM!

BUT-- HOW?!

ZEE CAPITAN DROPPED IT WHEN YOU DIVEBOMBED HIM! ZARAN SPOTTED IT!

SO WE HAVE TWO AND THEY HAVE TWO!

THAT MAKES IT IMPERATIVE WE--

ZEMOHHHH...

HERR MICAWBER, WHAT ARE YOU TRYING TO SAY, MEIN FREUND?

BEWARE... SOME ONE ELSE... WANTS THE STONE...

YES... YOU SAID THAT BEFORE! WHO? WHO?

WHAT'S THAT PSYCHIC SIMPLETON BLATHERING ABOUT NOW?

HOURS LATER...

THIS DOESN'T MAKE SENSE! SO FAR WE'VE LOCATED BLOODSTONE FRAGMENTS IN CAVERNS BENEATH MANHATTAN, THE AMAZON JUNGLE, THE BERMUDA TRIANGLE AND THE EGYPTIAN DESERT--

--ALL REMOTE AND SOLITARY PLACES. SO WHAT'S THE LAST PIECE DOING IN THE HEART OF TOKYO -- ONE OF THE MOST CROWDED PLACES ON EARTH?

I THINK YOU MISS ZEE SIGNIFICANCE OF ZEE FOUR SITES ZEE BLOODSTONES SECRETED ZEMSELVES, ZARAN. WHAT ZEY ALL HAD IN COMMON WAS ZAT ZEY WERE PLACES OF DEATH--

--ZEE CHAMBER OF ZEE CONSPIRACY, ZEE INCAN SACRIFICE WHEEL, ZEE SUNKEN AIRLINER, AND ZEE PHARAOH'S TOMB!

WHEREVER WE FIND ZEE FIFTH FRAGMENT, I WAGER WE WILL ALSO FIND A PLACE OF DEATH!

JUST SO IT'S NOT OURS, BATS!

I SAY WE JUST *TAKE THEM* FROM HIM!

YOU THINK HE EES *FOOLISH* ENOUGH TO BE *CARRYING* THEM?

HOW DID ZEMO *INTEND* TO GET HIM TO *SURRENDER* THE TWO FRAGMENTS HE HAS *ANYWAY*?

I DON'T *KNOW.* ZEE BARON TELLS US *NOTHING* SAVE WHAT HE *WEESHES* US TO DO!

LET'S *OVERPOWER* HIM AND TAKE HIM TO ZEMO!

CONSIDERING HOW *POORLY* WE FARED AGAINST HIM IN THE *PAST,* I DON'T THINK THAT IS A *VIABLE OPTION,* MON AMI.

LET ME CONTACT ZEMO AND SEE WHAT *HE* WOULD HAVE US DO.

FLIKLIK

AND SOON...

CAPITAN! ZEE BARONN SAYS I SHOULD GIVE YOU THIS *COMMUNICATOR.* WHEN YOU RETURN TO YOUR SHIP, CONTACT HIM AND HE WILL GIVE YOU DIRECTIONS WHERE TO *MEET* HIM. N'EST CE PAS?

UNDERSTOOD.

YOU GIVE YOUR *WORD* YOU WILL BRING YOUR *BLOODSTONE PIECES*?

YOU HAVE MY *WORD!*

HEY, CAPTAIN, WHERE'S YOUR *BIMBO*?

WE HAD A PARTING OF THE WAYS.

JERK! WHO'S HE CALLING A *BIMBO*?

MUSTN'T LET THEM SEE ME *LIMP* OR THEY MAY CHANGE THEIR MIND ABOUT *ATTACKING!*

TWO HOURS LATER...

GREAT *MEETING SITE*, THE LIP OF AN *INACTIVE* VOLCANO.

THERE'S *ZEMO'S* SHIP.

WONDER IF *DIAMONDBACK* MANAGED TO *STOW ABOARD* UNNOTICED--

--OR IF THEY *DISCOVERED* HER AND ARE HOLDING HER *HOSTAGE?*

I'D *BETTER* ASSUME I'M ON MY *OWN.*

ANYTHING *I* CAN DO, CAPTAIN?

JUST BE READY TO TAKE OFF AT A MOMENT'S NOTICE.

I DON'T SEE *DIAMONDBACK* AMONG THEM--

--BUT THAT DOESN'T MEAN THEY'RE NOT *HOLDING* HER---

--AS A *TRUMP CARD!*

THAT IS *CLOSE ENOUGH*, CAPTAIN!

DO YOU HAVE THE *GEMS?*

THEY'RE ABOARD MY *SHIP.*

TELL ME ZEMO, WHAT DO YOU INTEND TO *DO WITH* THEM?

NONE OF YOUR *BUSINESS.*

IF YOU DON'T *CLUE ME IN,* NEGOTIATIONS END *HERE,* MISTER.

NOT AT ALL, CAPTAIN! YOU HAVEN'T HEARD MY *TERMS!*

SURRENDER YOUR TWO GEM PIECES, OR--

--I BLOW UP A CITY BLOCK IN *DOWNTOWN TOKYO!*

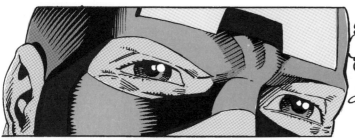

IS ZEMO *BLUFFING?* DID HE HAVE TIME TO PLANT EXPLOSIVES IN SOME BUILDING *BEFORE* THIS MEETING?

WOULD *DIAMONDBACK* HAVE *CAUGHT* HIM IF HE *HAD?*

I *EXPECTED* HIM TO HAVE FIGURED OUT SOME WAY TO *COERCE* WHAT HE WHAT HE WANTED OUT OF ME. I JUST DIDN'T KNOW PRECISELY WHAT IT WOULD *BE.*

WELL, CAPTAIN, I'M *WAITING.*

I'LL GIVE YOU *FIFTEEN SECONDS* TO MAKE UP YOUR MIND.

EINS.

ZWEI.

DREI.

VEIR.

MEANWHILE, ON ZEMO'S SHIP...

TALK ABOUT YOUR *ROUGH TRIPS.* CLINGING TO THIS CRAZY AIRCRAFT'S LANDING GEAR WITH *SUCTION-CUPS...*

...BREATHING THROUGH A *DIVING MASK...*

...GAMBLING THAT ZEEMY-BOY WOULDN'T FLY *TOO FAR* TO DO HIS *STONE-TRADING...*

...AND NOW SNEAKING ABOARD HIS SHIP WHILE HE AND THE BOYS ARE OUT *NEGOTIATING.*

LOOKS LIKE I'M ON A *ROLL.* NOW IF MY LUCK ONLY HOLDS OUT A LITTLE BIT LONGER, I'LL FIND OUT WHERE ZEMO HAS *HIS THREE STONES* STASHED WITHOUT TRIPPING AN *ALARM* OR ANYTHING--

--AND GET MY *PINK PAJAMAS* OUT OF HERE!

THEN CAP WILL BE FORCED TO ADMIT WHAT AN *ASSET* I AM TO HIM, AND--

--IS THAT A *COFFIN?*

YEP. AND INSIDE?

PHEEWWW! A VERY DEAD LOOKING *STIFF,* DRESSED IN A VARIATION OF *ZEMO'S DUD'S.*

WHO IS HE? HIS *BROTHER?* HIS *DAD?*

BACK OUTSIDE...

ALL RIGHT, ZEMO. I'LL GET MY *TWO GEMS.* WAIT HERE.

NO *TRICKS,* CAPTAIN-- OR *ELSE!*

I... LIVE... AGAIN!

MY GOD--THAT LOOKS LIKE ZEMO'S FATHER --ONE OF MY DEADLIEST ENEMIES--HEINRICH ZEMO! AND THE FIVE BLOODSTONE FRAGMENTS ARE ON HIS FOREHEAD!

SO THIS IS WHAT HE WANTED THE BLOODSTONE FOR!

VATER!

"VATER"? THAT MAN IN THE CENTER OF THE ELECTRICAL STORM IS HIS FATHER??

THAT INSIPID CAVE-DWELLER USED HIS POWER TO SCATTER MY SOUL-SHARDS ACROSS THIS PATHETIC PLANET...

--BUT I HAVE BEEN RE-STORED!

HE SEEMS TO BE SPEAKING OF ULYSSES BLOODSTONE, THE PREVIOUS POSSES-SOR OF THE GEM-- BUT WHY?

WHY DOES HE NOT SOUND LIKE MY BELOVED FATHER...

...AND HOW DID THE FIVE FRAGMENTS BECOME JOINED UPON HIS BROW??

BETTER TO DROP *NOW* THAN WHEN IT IS A THOUSAND FEET *HIGHER!*

HOLD ON, ZARAN-- I *HAVE* YOU!

I THINK I SEE A *PASSAGE DOWN*-- BUT IT'S GOING TO BE *TRICKY!*

COME TO ME, WEARISOME *GNAT!* LET YOURS BE THE FIRST MIND I *SUCK DRY!*

VAS?

THIS IS YOUR *FAULT*, CAPTAIN!

I COULD HAVE CONTROLLED THE BLOODSTONE'S *NECROMANCY* HAD YOU NOT *INTERFERED!*

NOT LIKELY, ZEMO!

SPDOOSH

A *GEYSER!*

HAD I BEEN A HAIR *SLOWER*--!

ZEMO, YOU MUST *HELP* ME ON THIS! WE MUST FIND A WAY TO *BREAK APART* THE BLOODSTONE OR ELSE--

NEIN! THIS IS MY ONLY CHANCE TO RAISE MY *VATER*--

--THE MAN *YOU* KILLED!

BDAM BDAM

THAT'S *NOT* HOW IT *HAPPENED*, ZEMO!

A FEW HOURS LATER...

GOOD DEAL.

OUTTA MY WAY *RUNTS!* I NEED TO BORROW YER *TUNA BOAT!*

SO WHAT DO WE GOT *HERE?* A *JAPANESE FISHIN' VILLAGE,* HUH?

BDAK

BDAK

WHOUL!

NNGHH!!

SMART FELLOW.

AIIEHH!

STUPID FELLOW.

SAYONARA, SUCKERS!

<HE FIGHTS LIKE A--A *DEMON!*>

<STOP HIM!>

<HOW? HE IS TOO *STRONG!*>

A SHORT TIME LATER, AT *AVENGERS ISLAND* IN NEW YORK HARBOR...

FLAGSHIP-ONE INITIATING LANDING PROCEDURES...!

CAP'N AMERICA! COLONEL JAMESON! HOW'D IT GO!?

HOW'D THE FLAG-SHIP HOLD UP ON HER *MAIDEN RUN?*

THE FLAGSHIP DID *ADMIRABLY,* MICHAEL.

AND *WE* MANAGED TO THWART MY OLD ENEMY, *BARON ZEMO,* FROM GETTING HIS MITTS ON THE *BLOODSTONE.*

I'M HITTING THE *SHOWERS,* CAPTAIN, AFTER ALMOST A *WEEK* COOPED UP IN THAT SHIP --*NNH*-- MY JUMPSUIT CAN ALMOST JUMP BY *ITSELF!*

WHILE YOU WERE AWAY I RAN A *SECURITY CHECK* ON THAT *WOMAN* YOU BROUGHT LAST WEEK, CAP'N.

DIAMOND-BACK.

NONE OTHER. SHE'S GOT A PRETTY SHADY *PAST.* POLICE BLOTTER SHOWS A LOT OF *ARRESTS* BUT NO *CONVICTIONS.* SHE'S A PRETTY BIG *SECURITY RISK.* I HOPE YOU'RE NOT PLANNING TO--

THANKS, MICHAEL.

UH, JUST DOIN' MY *JOB,* CAP'N.

SAY, *PEGGY...*

...ANY *MESSAGES* FROM THAT LADY I LEFT HERE WITH-- DIAMONDBACK?

NOT A *ONE,* STEVE.

I'LL BE IN MY *QUARTERS* IF YOU HEAR ANYTHING.

ODD SHE HASN'T BEEN IN TOUCH YET. CONSIDERING HOW LONG IT TOOK US TO GET BACK, WHAT WITH THAT PIT STOP IN EGYPT TO TELL THE MUMMY I LOST THE BLOODSTONE.

WHAT *HAPPENED* TO HER? WE SPLIT UP IN *TOKYO* SO SHE COULD KEEP AN EYE ON *ZEMO.* WASN'T SHE ABLE TO SNEAK ABOARD HIS *SHIP* AS PLANNED? HE DIDN'T *MENTION* HER.

LATER...

DON'T *FLATTER* YOURSELF, SISTER. WHAT WOULD MY BOSS DO WITH A SORRY PIECE OF STREETMEAT LIKE *YOU?*

THEN *WHAT?*

THAT'S FOR *ME* TO KNOW AND *YOU* TO FIND OUT.

WISECRACK WHILE YOU *CAN*, GHOULIE. SOON AS I GET THIS *ACID-DIAMOND* OUT OF MY *BOOT HEEL*--

OH, CRUD! HE MUST'VE *FOUND* IT!

YOU REALLY KNOW WHERE YOU'RE *GOING*, OR ARE YOU AS *LOST* AS YOU *LOOK?*

EVER HEAR OF A PLACE CALLED *MADRIPOOR?*

GEOGRAPHY WASN'T MY BEST SUBJECT.

WEIRD. THE MORE I *HEAR* IT, THE MORE THIS GUY'S *VOICE* SOUNDS *FAMILIAR!*

AVENGERS ISLAND...

I CAN'T SEEM TO STOP THINKING ABOUT *DIAMONDBACK*... WHEN SHE BROUGHT THE BLOODSTONE AFFAIR TO MY ATTENTION, I CONSIDERED HER QUITE A *NUISANCE*...

...BUT I HAVE TO ADMIT SHE'S BEEN QUITE AN *ASSET*, MANAGING TO GET HOLD OF SOME OF THE FRAGMENTS EVEN I WASN'T ABLE TO...

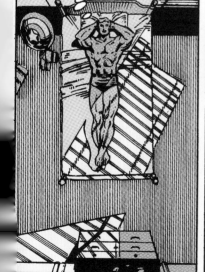

"*QUITE A CONTRAST FROM THE FIRST FEW TIMES WE MET. TWICE SHE WAS UNDER ORDERS FROM HER SERPENT SOCIETY CRONIES TO KILL ME, BUT SHE HELD BACK.*

"*OUR THIRD ENCOUNTER WE WORKED TOGETHER BRIEFLY, TRYING TO LOCATE THE SCOURGE OF THE UNDERWORLD. HER CONDUCT WAS WAY OUT OF LINE.*

AND NOW... WE NOT ONLY WORKED TOGETHER QUITE *WELL*, BUT I FIND MYSELF ALMOST *MISSING* HER.

SHE'S NOT MY *TYPE* AT ALL. SO HOW COME I CAN'T GET HER OUT OF MY *HEAD?*

AND...

TA-DAA! YER HOME AWAY FROM HOME!

LEMME HELP YOU GET COMFORTABLE!

I HEAR A SQUAWK OUTTA YOU, I'LL STRING YOU FROM THE CEILING FAN, DIG?

I DIG.

EASY NOW, THE MOMENT HE UNCUFFS YOUR HANDS--

GOT 'IM!

JAB

AHHH!

GOT HIS CROSSBOW!

G☆#☒▼!

TOSS ME THE KEYS, OR YOU GET THE SHAFT!

YOU WOULDN'T DO THAT.

YOU DON'T KNOW ME, PAL!

Ah, BUT I DO... RATSEL!

"RATSEL"! NO ONE'S CALLED ME THAT SINCE--

WHA-- DISTRACTED ME!

YOU PICKED A SORRY PLACE TO HIDE - CROSS!

WHAT HAPPENED...? I DIDN'T HEAR THE BOLT HIT THE FLOOR, BUT I DIDN'T HEAR CROSS-BONES CRY OUT EITHER!

SO SILENT... IT'S SCARY! WISH I HAD ANOTHER SHAFT!

BTCHHW

PRETTY VICIOUS, RATSEL--

THUPP

OHMI-GOD!

--BUT NOT VICIOUS ENOUGH!

Oh!

WHAT!

I COULD HAVE IMBEDDED THAT IN YOUR FORE-HEAD! NOW GIVE ME THAT BOW.

SOON AS YER NICE AN' SNUG, WE'RE MAKIN' A PHONE CALL TO YER NEW BOYFRIEND, CAPTAIN AMERICA-

SO THAT'S IT! I'M BAIT TO LURE HIM INTO A TRAP!

LIVE BAIT... AS LONG AS YOU DON'T HONK ME OFF AGAIN.

AVENGERS ISLAND...

CALL FOR YOU, STEVE. SOME GUY CLAIMING TO KNOW WHERE DIAMONDBACK IS!

PATCH HIM THROUGH!

YES?

GOT YER CHICK, DIAMOND-BACK. YOU WANT TO SEE HER ALIVE AGAIN YOU'LL HAUL YER STAR-SPANGLED BUTT TO MADRIPOOR--

--AND FIND THE BRASS MONKEY SALOON!

HOW DO I KNOW YOU HAVE--

CAP! DON'T! IT'S A TRAP! HE'S--

SHUT UP!!

WHO IS THIS? HELLO? HELLO?!

SOON...

SORRY TO GET YOU UP AT THIS HOUR, COLONEL -

IT'S OKAY. I'M A LIGHT SLEEPER.

OH, BEFORE WE FLY OUR SECOND MISSION TOGETHER, MIND CALL-ING ME "JOHN"? IT FEELS ODD HAVING A HIGHER "RANK" THAN YOU, ME BEING YOUR PILOT AND ALL--

I'LL TRY.

SO-- JOHN-- EVER BEEN TO MADRIPOOR?

THE PLACE IN QUESTION...

OKAY, THE BIG BOY SCOUT IS ON HIS WAY.

I'VE GOT SOME STUFF TO ARRANGE.

MMMPH!!

BE REAL GOOD.

NOW THAT THE TRAP IS SET, YER EXPENDABLE.

COCKY SON OF A SO-AND-SO!

SLAM

I'VE GOT TO FIND A WAY OUT OF HERE!

NNNYII! I'VE GOT A FEELING MY WRISTS WILL GIVE BEFORE THESE HANDCUFFS DO!

HOW STURDY IS THIS BED?

BDMPP

INDUSTRIAL STRENGTH. I GUESS IT HAS TO BE.

NOW WHAT? I CAN'T STAY HERE AND BE VICTIMIZED--NOT BY HIM OF ALL PEOPLE!

I CAN'T LET HIM TURN ME INTO A LIABILITY FOR CAP, EITHER!

I'VE GOT TO--

--FOOTSTEPS!

SOMEONE'S COMING!

HEY! HELP ME! **HELP ME!!**

PLEASE, YOU MUST HELP ME GET *FREE.* CROSSBONES IS A *MANIAC.* HE MEANS TO *KILL* ME! PLEASE -- *LIA,* ISN'T IT?

GET ME A *SAW* OR A *FILE* OR--

LIA, YOU HAVE A *CLIENT* WAITING. *GO!*

YES, MADAM.

ACHH!

MR. BONES SAY IF YOU MAKE DISTURBANCE, I TO *GAG* YOU.

CAN'T HAVE YOU ANNOY *CUSTOMERS.*

NO--WAIT! I *PROMISE* I'LL--

MMMPH!!

ONCE YOU *HOUSEBROKEN,* YOU MAKE GOOD *ADDITION* HERE. SOME CLIENTS GO FOR *EXOTIC* TYPES!

AFTER CROSS-BONES, YOU'RE GETTING *YOURS,* LADY!

WHO AM I KIDDING? WHAT CHANCE DO I HAVE TO *ESCAPE?*

BLOCKS AWAY...

DUNNO WHY I'M *RUSHIN'*, CAPTAIN A. WON'T BE HERE FOR *HOURS.*

GUESS I'M JUST ANXIOUS TO HAVE A SHOW-DOWN WITH A *WORTHY OPPONENT* FOR ONCE--

-- AROUND *THIS* NECK O' THE WOODS THERE AIN'T NOTHIN' BUT *WUSSES, WEENIES* AND *WIMPS!*

THINK I'LL SET MY FIRST TRAP *HERE.*

ALL I CAN SAY IS THE BOSS HAD BETTER *APPRECIATE* ALL THIS. WHEN IT COMES TO *VIOLENCE* I'M A REGULAR *REMBRANDT!*

MEANWHILE...

MANAGED TO ROCK THE BED TO POSITION MY HANDS UNDER THE *BOLT* BETTER...

JUST WISH THERE WAS *ROOM* TO SQUEEZE MY HAND THROUGH THE *BED-POST* HERE TO GIVE MY OTHER HERE A LITTLE MORE *SLACK!*

STILL...

...CAN'T...

...QUITE...

...REACH IT...

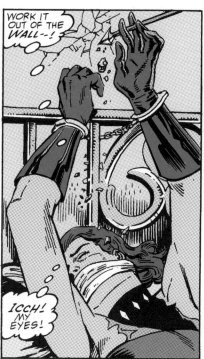

THE BRASS MONKEY...

BDAM
BDASH

KiiASHH

AN' *STAY OUT, YA WELSHER!*

Uhhll!...

NICE PLACE.

WHAT'LL IT *BE,* BLUE-MASK?

WANT THE TEENSY *UMBRELLA* THAT GOES WITH IT?

MINERAL WATER, PLEASE.

KEEP IT.

LOOKIN' FER THE *DIAMOND GIRL,* SPORT?

PAY MY TAB AND FOLLA ME.

THIS OUT-OF-SHAPE PUG DOESN'T SOUND LIKE THE GUY I SPOKE TO ON THE *PHONE.* MUST BE ONE OF HIS *STOOGES!*

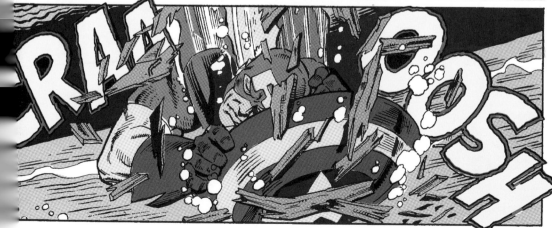

"SOMEPLACE *REAL SECURE*, CAP OL' CHAP. SOMPLACE YOU AIN'T GONNA *FIND* 'NLESS YER REAL *NICE* TA ME!"

OKAY, SO I MANAGED TO SLIP OUT OF CROSSBONES' LITTLE *LOCK-UP* AND FORCE HIS LADY FRIEND TO TELL ME WHICH WAY HE *WENT*--

--THE QUESTION IS, CAN I FIND *CAP* BEFORE MADAM XIANA'S *GOON SQUAD* FINDS ME--?

HEY-- WUZZA??

OOLPS!

WATCH WHERE YA--

YO, EDDIE, A *SKIRT!*

GUY ON THE *BIKE'S* BEEN *FOLLOWING ME* FOR BLOCKS!

I T'OUGHT DAT BUMP FELT *GOOSHY.*

WOOIE-- A *LOOKER*, TOO! A *PROFESSIONAL*, I'LL BET!

HEY, NOT SO *FAST*, TOOTSIE-- YA DIDN'T *'POLOGIZE* YET!

GOTCHA!

NOW HOW'BOUT A FREE *SAMPLE A' YER WARES?*

SAMPLE *THIS!*

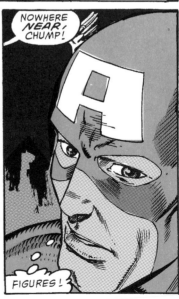

ELSEWHERE...

WELL, I'VE FINALLY *FOUND* THE PLACE. REMAINS TO BE SEEN IF CAP'S *SHOWN UP* YET.

THE ONLY WAY TO BE SURE IS TO GO IN AND *CHECK IT OUT.*

BUT SOMEHOW I GOT THE FEELING THE PLACE IS SWARMING WITH THE MADAM'S *HIRED THUGS.*

SO *NOW* WHAT? WISH I COULD CONTACT ONE OF MY CRONIES IN THE *SERPENT SOCIETY,* BUT BY THE TIME THEY SHAGGED HALF-WAY ACROSS THE *WORLD,* I'M SURE IT WOULD BE *TOO LATE.*

SO I GUESS ALL I CAN DO NOW IS COOL MY SPIKEY *HEELS* TILL I SPOT *CAP* OR THE HEAT'S OFF OR *SOMETHING...*

WAIT--DO I *HEAR*--?

AACK!!

YOU VERY *BAD LADY.* MADAM XIANA WANT YOU *DEAD.*

MISTER *PHUN* HAPPY TO OBLIGE!

AACCCK!

MY *THROAT!* NEARLY *CHOKED--!*

YOU *TRICKY LADY. MISTER PHUN* NOT LIKE TRICKS.

ALL OUT OF *THROWING DIAMONDS!* HAVE TO FIND A WEAPON--! THIS *PIPE--?*

MORE YOU MAKE ME *ANGRY,* MORE YOU WILL *SUFFER!*

THIS IS ONE *TOUGH GOON.* BETTER PUT SOME SPACE BETWEEN US, GIVE MY *TRACHEA* A CHANCE TO *RECOVER!*

MEANWHILE...

FIRST ORDER OF BUSINESS: DETERMINING WHETHER THERE REALLY *IS* A PRESSURE-SENSITIVE *PLATE* UNDER THIS PERSIAN RUG.

HMMM... THERE IS A SECTION OF FLOORBOARD ABOUT FOUR BY FOUR FEET THAT'S *SEPARATED* FROM THE REST-- PROBABLY *IS* WHAT BONES SAID.

WONDER IF HE RAN *AROUND* THE RUG, OR ACTIVATED IT AFTER HE RAN ACROSS --- WITH THE *LIGHT SWITCH* FOR INSTANCE.

NO WAY TO TELL FROM *HERE*.

WONDER IF THE BOMB IS *UNDER* THESE FLOORBOARDS, OR JUST THE *TRIGGER-MECHANISM*...

THAT SMALL *SLOT* NEAR THE CEILING ON THE FAR WALL-- AN *OBSERVATION WINDOW?*

HMMM... IF BONES HAS SOME *GOON* OBSERVING ME, IT TELLS ME *TWO THINGS*:

ONE, THAT THE BOMB IS *NOT* SO POWERFUL THAT AN *OBSERVER* HAS TO FEAR FOR HIS *LIFE*...

TWO, THE BOMB IS AS *CLOSE TO ME* AND AS FAR AWAY FROM THE OBSERVATION SLOT AS POSSIBLE.

WAIT! THERE'S *ANOTHER* POSSIBILITY! BONES MAY CONSIDER HIS OBSERVER... *EXPENDABLE.*

CUT: YO, BOSS, THIS IS CROSSBONES. I'VE GOT SOME *GOOD NEWS* AND SOME *BAD NEWS.*

THE *BAD* IS I DON'T HAVE THE *BLOODSTONES,* ON THE OTHER HAND, *NOBODY* DOES. ZEMO FELL DOWN A *VOLCANO* WITH 'EM. *

*REFERENCES TO OUR MINI-SAGA IN CAP #357-362. --RALFSTONE

CROSSCUT: WELL, *ONE* THING'S FOR SURE. I'M NOT *ACCOMPLISHING* ANYTHING STANDING AROUND HERE.

TIME TO *TRY* SOMETHING!

CUT: THE GOOD NEWS IS I'VE CAPTURED YOUR GREATEST ENEMY, CAPTAIN AMERICA! SO WHAT DO YOU WANT I SHOULD *DO* WITH HIM??

YOU DID *WHAT?* YOU *FOOL!* LET HIM *GO!*

CROSSCUT: IF I'M RIGHT, AND THE BOMB ITSELF IS UNDER THE *FLOORBOARDS,* MY SHIELD SHOULD TAKE THE *BRUNT* OF THE EXPLOSION.

CUT: YOU ARE MY *SECRET WEAPON,* CROSSBONES! I DO NOT WANT YOU TO GET MIXED UP WITH *HIM* UNLESS I *ORDER* YOU TO DO SO!

NOW *DROP* WHAT YOU'RE DOING AND *RETURN* TO ME AT ONCE! *UNDERSTAND?!*

CROSSCUT: STEADY NOW. ON THE COUNT OF *THREE,* I'LL *JUMP!*

CUT:

GO FIGURE. MAN, IF I DIDN'T NEED MY *LIFE* SO BADLY, I'D BE TEMPTED TO *DISOBEY* THE BOSS NOW AND THEN!

CROSSCUT:

ONE...

TWO...

THREE...

CUT:

HEY, MAYBE CAPPY'LL GET SO TIRED WAITIN' FER ME TO *RETURN*, HE'LL *BLOW Y'MSELF UP*!

BOSS CAN'T *BLAME* ME FOR *THAT*, CAN HE?

CROSSCUT:

JUMP!

WABOOM

CUT:

Yeehahhh! HE DID IT! THAT IMPATIENT OL' SUNUVAGUN BLEW HIMSELF UP!

HA HA HA

NEARBY...

AN EXPLOSION...? SOUNDED... SO CLOSE...

OH, PLEASE, LET IT HAVE NOTHING TO DO WITH CAP!

AND SOON...

CAN'T TELL A THING. THE BUILDING'S STILL ON FIRE!

DON'T THEY HAVE A FIRE DEPARTMENT IN THIS STINKING TOWN??

DIAMOND-BACK?

CAP!!

Whuff!

Uh, IT'S GOOD TO SEE YOU, TOO. I SEE YOU'RE FREE. GUESS I CAME ALL THIS WAY TO RESCUE YOU FOR NOTHING.

OFFER A GIRL A LIFT HOME?

SURE. SOON AS WE SCOUR THIS BURG FOR A PUG-UGLY NAMED CROSSBONES.

SAY, CAP... IS THIS THE BEGINNING OF A BEAUTIFUL FRIENDSHIP..?

I'LL HAVE TO GET BACK TO YOU ON THAT.

End